Rose and Sebastian

Cynthia Zarin

Illustrated by Sarah Durham

Houghton Mifflin Company Boston 1997

For information about this and other Houghton Mifflin
trade and reference books and multimedia products,
visit The Bookstore at Houghton Mifflin on the
World Wide Web at http://www.hmco.com/trade/.

The text of this book is set in 16 point New Caledonia.
The illustrations are gouache and ink, reproduced in full color.

Library of Congress Cataloging-in-Publication Data

Zarin, Cynthia.
Rose and Sebastian/by Cynthia Zarin; illustrated by Sarah Durham.
p. cm.
Summary: Rose is frightened by the noises coming from the apartment
upstairs, but then she and her mother pay a visit to the boy who lives there.
ISBN 0-395-75920-X
[1. Noise — Fiction. 2. Fear — Fiction. 3. Apartment houses — Fiction.]
I. Durham, Sarah, ill.   II. Title.
PZ7.Z263R0 1997 [E] — dc20 95-16367
CIP AC

Manufactured in the United States of America
BVG 10 9 8 7 6 5 4 3 2 1

For Rose Cornelia Seccareccia
and Sebastian Bonfante Raditsa

— C.Z.

For my Dad

— S.D.

Rose lives in an apartment in New York City. From her window she can see cars, dogs, people, airplanes, and delivery vans. Sometimes she can see fire engines. Across the park she can see the elevated train. In winter she sees a snowplow. In summer she sees the ice cream man. In summer the fountain across the street is turned on and she can see that too. All of these things make noise: **HONK HONK WOOF BARK CHATTER BANG WHOOSH WHOOSH RING-A-LING SWISH SWISH.**

But nothing makes more noise than Sebastian.
Sebastian lives upstairs.

When Rose was smaller than she is now,
she wasn't afraid of cars honking and
dogs barking or the ice cream man.

She was afraid of Sebastian.
When Rose was smaller than
she is now she couldn't
say "Sebastian."
She said "Martian."

Everyone thought this was very funny. When
Sebastian's friend Pete heard about it, he fell
down laughing in the elevator.
 Still, he didn't make as much noise as Sebastian.

ZOW WHEE ZOW WHEE ZOW WHEE went
the noise over Rose's head while she was eating her
lunch.

"That?" she asked her mother.

"That's just Sebastian," her mother said.

ARRGH ARRGH ARRGH Rose heard while she was taking her bath. She jumped right out of the tub and ran down the hall without a towel.

"That?" asked Rose when her mother caught up with her.

"Oh, it's just Sebastian," said her mother.

"Scared," said Rose. Then she got into her pajamas.

TIP PAT TIP PAT TIP PAT TIP PAT. It was a rainy Saturday, and Rose was listening to the wet song the rain was singing on the window. She was building a city.

ZOW WHEE ZOW WHEE ZOW WHEE came the noise from upstairs.

"Oh, my goodness, that Sebastian!" said Rose's mother.

But that day Rose, who was feeling brave, looked up at the ceiling, where there was an eensy water stain in the shape of a cloud, and said, "I want to see."

"You want to see Sebastian?" asked her mother.
"Yes," said Rose.

So Rose's mother called Sebastian's mother on the telephone and asked if Rose could come and visit before supper.

All afternoon, while Rose drew pictures and read books and finished her city, whenever she heard **ZOW WHEE ZOW WHEE ZOW WHEE,** she looked up at the ceiling and said, "Soon."

At five o'clock Rose and her mother took the elevator upstairs to visit Sebastian.

The door to Sebastian's apartment was blue, just
like Rose's door.
    "Knock," said Rose's mother.
Rose knocked.
The door opened.

There was Sebastian.
"Hi Rose," he said.
Rose was very quiet.
But not Sebastian.
**"ZOW WHEE ZOW
WHEE ZOW WHEE,"**
yelled Sebastian as
he raced down the hall.

"ARRGH ARRGH ARRGH,"
he growled at the mirror on the bathroom
door, sticking out his tongue and showing
his teeth at the same time.
　　Rose started to laugh.

THUNK THUNK THUNK went Sebastian's
basketball as he bounced it on the kitchen floor.
"Roll it back, Rose," said Sebastian.
Rose rolled the ball back.

Then Sebastian showed her his toy forest, his cat, Long Ears, and his new helicopter. Even though it was time for supper, Rose's mother and Sebastian's mother had tea, and everyone had some delicious cake with raisins in it.

Then it was time to go.

THUNK THUNK THUNK came the noise from
upstairs when Rose sat down to eat her supper.

   "WOO WOO WOO, MARTIAN," shouted Rose,
shaking her spoon at the ceiling.

   "Scared?" asked her mother.

   "No!" said Rose.

That night, after she had had her bath and her bedtime drink, and her mother had sung her a song and said good night, Rose lay in her bed, listening.

Upstairs there was one tiny bang, then another. **"GOODNIGHT, MARTIAN!"** Rose shouted. **"WOO WOO WOO WOO!"**

And Sebastian, who was just getting ready for bed,
was so surprised that his mother had to tuck him
in three times that night before he could fall asleep.